Can't you sleep, Piglittle?

Sally Grindley • Andy Ellis

Piglittle rolled over and over and tried to go to sleep.

"I'm too cold, Mummy," he whimpered.

Primrose Pig covered him with straw.
"Sleep tight, my poppet," she said.

"I'm too hot now," cried Piglittle.
He jumped up and pushed away
the straw.

Primrose Pig began to snore. "Oh no," squealed Piglittle. "I'll never get to sleep."

He crept out of the pen and
scampered off round the farmyard
to see if anyone else was awake.

First he peeped through the henhouse window, but the hens were all asleep.

Then he ran down to the pond to see Dabble Duck, and squealed with delight.

"Wake up, Dabble!" he squeaked.
"The moon has fallen into your pond!
Let's catch it."

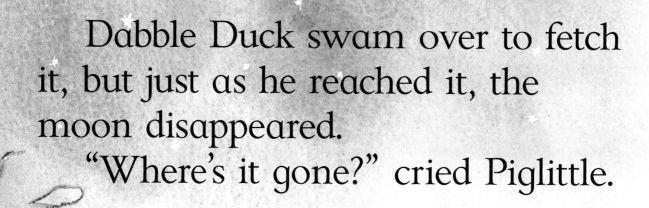

Dabble Duck swam over to fetch
it, but just as he reached it, the
moon disappeared.
"Where's it gone?" cried Piglittle.

"The fish must have taken it," said Dabble Duck. He paddled round and round, but couldn't see it anywhere.

"Let's wait for them to bring it back," yawned Piglittle.

He lay down and rested his chin on his trotters. Dabble Duck sat down beside him. Soon they were fast asleep.

Piglittle was woken by a wet kiss. "I've been looking for you everywhere," said Primrose Pig.